J

The
Homework
MYSTERY

The

Homework
MYSTERY

M. MITNSI

Note: This is a work of fiction. Names, characters, businesses, places, events and incidents are either the products of the author's imagination or used in a fictitious manner. Any resemblance to actual persons, living or dead, or actual events is purely coincidental.

First Edition: August 2015

ISBN 13: 978-1516978571
ISBN 10: 1516978579

Cover design by M. Mitnsi

1.

I was so proud of my homework. I finished it early. It was my best work ever. I made sure to put it in my backpack before I went to sleep. I didn't want to forget it at home and be in trouble the next day at school.

"Kendra," my mom said as she woke me up. "It's time to go to school."

I yawned. My mom helped me get out of bed. I didn't like getting out of bed.

***

School: The Classroom

"Hey, Kendra," Neal said as he hit my backpack. I turned around and gave Neal a mean look. He started laughing. I smiled.

"Did you get your homework done?" I asked. "It was actually fun. I finished my story early. My mom loved it."

"Yeah," Neal said. "I wrote about a superhero. He saved the world from evil people like you."

I laughed. "Whatever," I said.

After taking off my backpack and sitting down next to Neal, Catalina sat on my other side.

"Hey, girl," she said. "What did you write about?"

"Everyone settle down," our teacher,

Mrs. King, said, interrupting us. "Now it's time for your favorite part of the day. Everyone pass up your homework."

I was proud as I picked up my backpack and searched through it. I knew Mrs. King would love my story.

At first I couldn't find my homework. I remembered putting it in my orange folder but it wasn't there.

I looked into my bag again. There it was. The purple folder, the one I might have put my homework into. I took it out, put it on my desk, but when I opened it, my work was gone!

"What." I whispered. "No way!"

I pulled all of my folders out of my backpack. After going through each of them, I still couldn't find it!

"Now, kids, stop playing," Mrs. King

said. "Pass up your homework."

I looked up and saw that everyone was in the same situation as me. Some of my classmates threw their hands up. Some looked confused. They couldn't find their homework either.

"Why hasn't anyone passed up their homework?" Ms. King asked. She sounded a little more irritated than before.

"I can't find mine," all of my classmates said in one way or another.

I knew I had my homework, so I looked through my folders again. Nothing.

"This is so strange," Neal whispered to me. "I knew I put it in my bag."

"So did I," I said.

Uh oh. Mrs. King walked over to me. "Kendra, stop talking. Where is your homework?"

"I'm sorry, Mrs. King," I said. "I put my homework in my bag last night. I don't know what happened!"

Mrs. King squinted then went back to the front of the class. "Is this a joke?" she asked.

"No!" all of the kids in my class said.

"Is this opposite day?" Mrs. King said.

"No!" we said.

"Well, it looks like I will be talking to all of your parents. And you will all need to do another assignment. I will not tolerate these games in my class." Mrs. King was furious.

"But, Mrs. King," Catalina said.

"There will be more homework," Mrs. King said. "And it will be due next week. No games," she said in a harsh voice.

The classroom was silent. Everyone was scared to talk. Even Ryan, who asked questions about everything, didn't dare raise his hand. We knew we were in deep trouble.

Mrs. King started out class giving us an even harder homework assignment. It wasn't fair. It wasn't our fault our homework was gone.

2.

Recess

I couldn't wait to get to recess. I was just glad we got to have one. Mrs. King sure was mad. If she were a cartoon, she would have had steam coming out of her nose and mouth. She might have even turned into the Hulk.

"It wasn't right," Neal complained as he, Catalina, Tyrone, and I barely hit the tether-ball. Usually, tether-ball was our favorite game. We had competitions and everything. That day we were just so sad we couldn't play.

"I agree," Catalina said. "She didn't even give us the chance to explain."

"Well, she does think we all planned it," Tyrone said. He was the unlucky one who sat across the class from us.

"But how could that be?" I asked, throwing my hands up. "Most of us don't even get along!"

"I know!" Neal said.

"What if someone did this?" Catalina said. "As a joke."

"How could that even be humanly possible?" Neal asked.

"It can't," Tyrone said. "Unless…"

"There's no way," I said. "No way."

"Odd stuff happens on the *Strange Things* show," Tyrone said. He raised his eyebrows and a smile spread across his face.

"That's fake!" Catalina said.

"Duh," Neal said. "But this is real."

We hit the ball a couple of times before I looked into the field and saw a piece of torn paper. It looked like part of the drawing from my assignment. We not only wrote a story but had to draw a picture to show a scene from it.

I breathed in quickly and ran to the paper.

"Kendra!" Neal said then ran after me. Catalina and Tyrone followed.

I picked up the paper and it *was* from my homework. I looked up again and saw another piece and ran to it.

"Wait!" Catalina said.

Catalina, Neal, and Tyrone caught up to me when I picked up the second piece of paper. We were on the edge of the school playground, right next to the tall fence that was covered by plants.

"You guys," I said and turned around. I held up the two small pieces of paper. The second one wasn't from my homework, but had Tyrone's name on it.

"Hey, that's my name!" Tyrone said. He grabbed the paper from me. Neal took the other piece.

"You know what this means," Catalina said.

"Yeah," Tyrone said. "That *Strange Things* show isn't so fake after all."

3.

"We need to find out what happened," I said.

"Yeah, then we would be the heroes of our school!" Neal said.

"I just want to find out so we won't have to do another assignment," Catalina said.

"So where do we start?" Tyrone asked.

"Well," I said. "It seems like whoever took it either wanted us to find it, or didn't know that it dropped."

"I wonder why they would tear it up though," Neal said.

"That's what I'm thinking too," Tyrone said. "Could it be someone from another class? Someone with some type of superpower?"

"That's not possible," Catalina said.

"It has to be possible," Neal said.

I nodded. "They had to take it sometime before we got to school. Unless they could turn invisible and reach into our backpacks...and make our homework invisible."

"I can't believe we are even thinking about this," Catalina said. "Invisible people."

"Well, a spell..." Tyrone said.

"Wait!" Catalina said. "Like I was saying, what if the joke was on us? What if

Mrs. King and our parents decided to teach us something by taking our homework?"

"That makes a lot of sense," I said.

"And it's not supernatural!" Catalina said. "It has to be that."

"You're a genius, Catalina!" Neal said.

"Aww," Tyrone said. "You're right. But I was hoping it could be something they would put on *Strange Things*."

"Tyrone!" we said.

"What?" Tyrone said.

We turned around to start walking toward the school, back to the playground area. The bell was about to ring.

With every step I took I had a growing desire to look back to the fence. A bizarre feeling, like someone or something was watching us, kept bothering me. I turned and saw someone peeking in between the trees and plants that covered the gates.

It looked like another kid, our same age, but the kid had big light-purple eyes. On top of that he didn't have a black spot in the center of his eyes, no pupils. I closed my eyes and shook my head then looked again. The kid was gone! I had to be imagining it.

Catalina grabbed my arm, and I jumped.

"Are you okay?" Catalina asked.

"Yeah," I said. "I'm just imagining things."

***

As we walked in line back to class, I bent over to Neal and said, "So, do we tell Mrs. King we think it is a joke on us?"

"Absolutely not!" Neal said. "Did you

see her before? She was angry. And what if Catalina was wrong? Telling Mrs. King would make things worse."

Catalina spun around. "I heard my name," she said.

"We were just saying we should ask our parents first," I said.

"Good idea," Catalina said.

***

We spent the rest of the school day letting our class know that we thought the disappearance of our homework was a joke on us. By the end of the day, everyone agreed to ask their parents when they got home.

4.

I was so glad when school was over. I just wanted to go somewhere else. Somewhere like the movies. Somewhere so I could forget what was happening.

Catalina, Neal, and I walked together down the sidewalk looking for our parents' cars. We were almost to the fence next to the school field when I saw him.

It was the same boy I saw at recess. I knew it had to be him. I saw that I was right when he looked over to us, and he had those big purple eyes.

"There he is!" I said, pointing.

"Who?" Catalina said before she saw him.

"How could his eyes be that big?" Tyrone asked.

I took a step forward, and the boy started walking fast in the other direction.

"Excuse me!" I shouted. "I just want to talk to you."

The boy started jogging. When I started jogging, he started running.

We couldn't keep up with the boy. By the time he got down the street, he got even faster. He ran at some super speed.

"No way!" I said, turning around to face my friends. "Did you just see that? He ran superfast. Faster than the fastest human!"

"Yeah!" Catalina and Neal said.

"*Strange Things* I tell you," Tyrone said. "Strange things. We have to get him on video!"

"*No!*" Catalina said. "That may scare him."

"It would," Neal said.

"We have to find him though," I said.

"Why?" Neal said.

"Look," I said and pointed toward the gate. "He was standing there this morning."

We walked over to the gate. There was a note tucked into the hole. I picked it up and read it out loud. It said, "We're sorry."

"We?" Neal said. "So there are more?"

"I have to admit something," Tyrone said.

"What?" I asked.

"I'm actually kind of scared now,"

Tyrone said.

I bit my lip.

"Me too," Catalina said.

Our frightening moment was interrupted by Catalina's mother calling out her name. She must have pulled up closer as the other cars left. Her car was right next to us, but we didn't even notice it. We nearly jumped onto the fence.

"What's wrong?" her mother yelled. "Are you all still going to the pool?"

"Oh yeah," I said.

"I totally forgot about it," Neal said.

"Yes, Mom," Catalina said. She turned to us. "Strategy session?"

We nodded.

After Catalina left, Tyrone's mother came then Neal's father. Neal asked me if I was going to be alright before he left. I told him I would. There were other kids there. But the truth was I was afraid that the boy would show up again. He wouldn't be alone that time. He would be with his family. All of them.

***

I knew I survived the most terrifying minutes of my life when my mom showed up a few minutes later.

"Did something happen at school today?" she asked me when I put on my seat belt.

"Uhh," I said. I didn't want to lie. I would get in even more trouble. "I didn't have my homework. No one had their homework. Something strange happened today."

"Huh," my mom said. "That is very strange."

"Yeah, and we got in trouble for it," I said. "We have even more homework to do this weekend."

"Well, maybe if you can find your homework, you can turn it in."

I started to get the feeling that my mom knew something about it. I thought she would have been mad. What if Catalina was right?

"Yeah," I said and looked out the window. "Maybe we can find it."

5.

The Swimming Pool

After jumping off the diving board, I swam over to where Catalina and Neal were, on the side of the pool. Tyrone joined us after diving in. That was part of our plan to distract our parents. Act like we were tired of jumping into the pool.

I was actually kind of surprised our parents still let us go to the pool knowing what happened in school. But when I looked at them, I saw why. They were the ones who wanted to go.

Neal's dad kept jumping off the diving board. The moms were busy gossiping while taking in some sun.

Catalina, Neal, Tyrone, and I formed ourselves into a circle and began to discuss our plans.

"Did you ask your parents about it?" I asked.

"No way," Neal said. "I didn't notice my dad acting strange. He just kept talking about how fun it was going to be at the pool."

"My mom was mad that Mrs. King thought we were playing a joke," Tyrone said.

"I asked my mom after telling her what

happened," Catalina said. "She laughed and said we have an active imagination. There was no way that she, or any parent, would do that. She is going to talk to Mrs. King on Monday."

I told my friends what happened to me.

"So that rules them out, for the most part," Tyrone said.

"Well, we know that the boy has something to do with it," Neal said.

"Yeah," I said. "He probably left the clues then watched us."

"Yes, he wanted to be found," Tyrone said. "But what if this is a coincidence? What if he is sorry for something else?"

"It could be," I said. "We still have to find him though."

"So how do we find him now?" Catalina asked.

"Good question," Neal said. "Online? Through a social media search?"

"But would he even have a profile?" I said. "And it's not like we could search for purple eyes."

"We could do just a regular search for people like him," Neal said. "Sightings of purple eyes."

"He sounds like an alien now," Catalina said. She shivered.

"What if he is an alien and not a superhuman?" I said.

"We would need to be more careful," Tyrone said. "Don't make him mad. A superhuman is still human. An alien is something else."

"But what if they were human aliens?" Neal said, raising his eyebrows.

"Well, we don't know what they are for

sure until we talk to one," Catalina said. "And I am not about to do that."

"Catalina, he was nice though," I said. "Well, he seemed nice. He did say they were sorry."

"Okay, so we know they could be nice and have purple eyes," Neal said.

"And they're superfast runners," I added. "But wait. We still have to consider our parents. My mom didn't seem to care that the homework was lost. The others could have been acting. What if..." I stared out onto the pool. "What if our parents turned into aliens?!"

"No!" Catalina said. "Don't say that!"

"It's possible," Tyrone said. "During some alien attacks they turn the humans into aliens."

"Then we're doomed," I said.

"Now wait a minute," Neal said. "Kendra, you were just saying they were nice. Now you're saying they could be evil?"

"Well, we don't know," I said.

"Which brings us back to our first point," Tyrone said. "How do we find them?"

"Are we sure we want to find them?" Catalina asked.

Neal's dad swam over to us. "Kids, what are you doing?" he asked. "We are at a pool. You are supposed to be having fun!"

"We are, Dad," Neal said.

"Well," his dad said. "It looks like you are having a serious conversation. Live a little. You will be sad when this fun part of your life is over." He started splashing us. At first the splashes were little then they got bigger.

"This is war!" Tyrone shouted, and we started splashing back.

After we played for a while, I had to go to the bathroom. I hated when that happened. I didn't want to get out of the pool.

6.

Walking to the bathroom was kind of creepy. It was under a covered area. Only a small amount of light reached the door. I hurried inside. At least it was fully lit.

As I exited the bathroom, I sensed someone watching me again. The sensation told me to look to my left. I did. And there those big purple eyes were!

I took a deep breath in. I was scared. Was he making me feel his presence?

"Don't be scared," the boy said. He reached out his hand toward mine. I touched his fingertip with my own then withdrew my finger quickly.

He laughed. "I'm not going to hurt you," he said. "I'm a kid. Just like you."

He held out his hand for me to shake it. "I'm—" The boy stopped before he said anything else. He looked alarmed and took off running around the back of the bathroom area.

I whipped my head back and saw Neal standing there with his mouth wide open.

My brain reminded me to stop standing there. Catch up to the boy. I started running.

"Don't run!" Neal yelled as he chased after me. "It's too slippery. You'll fall!"

It was too late. I slipped and was about to hit the ground. I would have fallen on my arm and knees, but I didn't. I felt cool arms catch me.

I glanced up. The boy was holding me.

"Gotta go. See you later," the boy said and sat me on the ground before he scurried away. Neal was at my side seconds later.

"Are you alright?" Neal asked. He grabbed my arms to pull me to my feet.

"Yeah," I said. "He spoke perfect English. He told me not to be scared. He caught me."

"Well, I'm just glad you're okay," Neal said.

"What happened?!" Catalina and Tyrone asked as they came around the corner.

"Kendra?" Catalina said.

"She might have just been the first human to have contact with an alien," Neal said. "Or the supernatural."

Tyrone and Catalina were in shock.

We spent the rest of the night talking about what happened over at Neal's house. His dad made everyone pizza. Then, on top of that, some of our moms made dessert. It was like they were being nice to us on purpose. Too nice.

This rarely happened unless there was a birthday or some sort of celebration. The changes in our parents' attitudes made us wary. We agreed to continue to monitor our parents for more changes. To keep ourselves safe, we also planned to get together to "do homework" every day until we had the mystery figured out.

7.

Saturday

Catalina, Tyrone, Neal, and I found ourselves at the library the next day to work on our new projects due on Friday. This wasn't a fake homework session. We really needed to get going.

Three weeks. That was the amount of time we would normally have for the type of project Mrs. King gave us.

I found the book I was looking for and joined my friends in a group room. That way we could talk.

"How are you feeling?" Tyrone asked me. "Did anything strange happen overnight?"

"No," I said as I took a seat.

"He could be turning you into one of them, you know," Tyrone said. "On this one movie—"

"Okay, Tyrone," Catalina said, interrupting him. "We get it. You saw a movie where stuff happened. It was probably based on one of the stories from *Strange Things*. They turned into monsters and they all died. But that was fake. This is real."

Tyrone came over to me and felt my forehead. "Well, at least she feels normal."

He picked up my hand and inspected my finger. "Her finger looks normal too."

"That's because I am normal," I said. "Look, if I turn into an alien. I'll let you know."

"Cool," Tyrone said and took his seat.

Neal gave him a strange look.

"What?" Tyrone asked.

"You guys, what if my mom was right though?" I said. "What if Mrs. King will cancel the new project if we find our homework—if we solve the mystery?"

"Then we don't have much time," Neal said. "Every day we don't know the truth is time we have to spend working on our project."

"But if our parents are in on it, then it will be almost impossible to find out what happened in time," Tyrone said. "I could see my mom keeping the secret until the day we turn our second project in. She would say we are smarter and better because of it."

"Yeah," Catalina said. "My mom would say the same thing."

"But how did they get my dad to agree?" Neal asked.

"Our moms asked him nicely," Tyrone said.

We laughed. Even though Neal's dad was pretty cool with us, our moms could be very persuasive.

"We should get to work on these reports," Neal said.

"Neal, you must be in on it," Tyrone said.

We laughed once more before we followed Neal's advice and opened our books to try to read for at least a few minutes. Most of the time when we worked as a group, someone was bound to interrupt the silence.

8.

Fifteen minutes later

"**M**an, I can't believe we are here doing homework again!" Tyrone said. "At least on the story we could make up something interesting. For this book report we have to read the book first then write."

"I know," Catalina said. "That's why I chose a short book."

"But even those short books on the list

weren't interesting," Neal said.

"Well, I tried to find—" I said, but stopped in the middle of the sentence. My eyes couldn't be tricking me. Through our group-room window, I saw the boy. He was far away from us and in the library too! He passed by. He was wearing sunglasses.

"What?" Catalina said, racing to my side to see what I saw. She looked over to me.

"It's the kid, isn't it?" Tyrone asked.

I nodded slowly.

"Well, if he's out there, we need to corner him or something," Neal said, standing up. "We need to find out what happened."

"Last time he ran when he saw you, Neal," I said. "Maybe I should ask him myself."

"We will keep our distance then," Neal said. "If you are in trouble, we'll help."

I was the first person go out of the group room. I crept over to the area where I saw the boy last then looked down the aisles. He wasn't there. I turned to my friends and shrugged.

Then I saw the boy walk down the science fiction aisle out of the corner of my eye. I walked over to the aisle, and there he was, looking at books about aliens.

"Hey," I whispered.

The boy looked at me then gasped. He put the book back then speed walked past me without saying anything. I followed him.

The boy looked over and saw Neal, Catalina, and Tyrone making their way toward him too. He started walking even faster toward the exit. I felt like running to try and keep up.

I knew it was wrong to leave. We would definitely get in trouble for leaving without telling our parents. The boy could have set a trap for us. But I had to find out what was going on.

As soon as I got out of the library, I took off running after the boy through the grass, toward the playground behind the building. The strange thing was the boy wasn't running as fast as he did before. I was five steps away from him when he stopped and turned around. I froze.

Immediately I could feel my heart pumping. Was this part of his plan—to get me away from the library then kidnap me?

Tyrone, Catalina, and Neal caught up to us and stood by my side. The boy took a step toward us, and we took a few steps back.

"Don't be afraid," the boy said. "I wanted to meet you. My name is Mye."

Mye reached out his hand to shake one of ours. I reached toward him, but Catalina pulled me back.

"He may be dangerous," she whispered into my ear.

"I don't want to hurt you," Mye said. "I would like to be your friend."

"Well, why did you show up the day someone took our homework?" Neal asked, crossing his arms.

"I had to give you the note," the boy said. "I wanted to talk to you, but y'all started walking away."

"Yeah. You left the note. Did you eat our homework?" Tyrone asked.

"And did you get our parents to help you?" Catalina said. "Did you turn them into someone else?"

Mye laughed. "No. I don't eat homework and I don't know your parents. I'm very sorry, but Max took your work. He took the papers from all of your classmates. I didn't notice that he was gone. He took my navigator and went to all of your houses at night. I caught him, drinking juice while he read your stories."

"Why would he want to do that?" I asked.

"He loves reading homework," Mye said.

My friends and I were puzzled as we looked at each other.

"He used to be a teacher when we lived on Martiana," Mye said.

"So you are an alien!" Tyrone said, pointing to him.

"Yes," Mye said.

"And you live here?" Catalina said.

"Yes, I was born here," Mye said.

"Interesting," Neal said. "So you have a family?"

"Yes, we live over there." Mye pointed to a house across the street.

"And you didn't come to hurt us?" Tyrone said.

"No," Mye said and started sniffling. "They make us look like we are all bad. Like we are evil."

"Are you okay?" I asked.

Before Mye could answer, a robotic-appearing dog ran toward us and jumped up on Mye. The dog started licking his arm. Mye smiled.

"This is Max," Mye said.

"What?!" my friends and I said.

"The same Max—" I said.

Max spun into the air and turned into a human-appearing robot then spun back around to look like a dog.

"Why yes," Max said.

Our mouths dropped open. The dog talked.

"Our dogs can talk like humans," Mye said, "because they can turn into a human. Their species likes to be a pet though. They love living with us."

"Whoa!" Tyrone said.

"Well, Max, do you have anything to say?" Mye said. "You took their homework."

"I'm sorry," Max said and looked to the ground. "But I just wanted to read the homework. I miss reading homework."

"Max, you could have read my work," Mye said.

"Okaay," Max said. "The real reason I took it is because Mye was sad that he couldn't play with the humans. He wanted to go to school, but Mom said no."

"Why can't you go to school?" I asked.

"Because I'm an alien. We are not allowed to go to school, and if I did, people would treat me differently," Mye said. "That's what Mom says."

"I hate to say it, but she's probably right," Catalina said. "There are some bullies."

"But it shouldn't stop you from going to school," I said. "What if they changed the rules?"

"Yeah," Neal said. "We could tell our parents—"

"Tell your parents what?" Neal's dad asked. My mom was walking up next to him with her arms crossed. We were in big trouble.

9.

My mom looked concerned when she saw Max. Then she looked over to Mye.

"Who is your new friend?" my mom asked.

We explained the situation to my mom and Neal's dad. They felt bad that Mye didn't get to go to school and weren't too mad that we left the library. They were also surprised that aliens did exist and lived with us for years.

All of us followed Mye to his house. We were nervous while we waited for Mye's parents to come to the door. Although Mye was very nice, we didn't know much about aliens. And most movies and books were about them attacking humans. I guess it affected us more than we thought.

We heard Mye's mom say, "You brought who?" She spoke English too.

I didn't know if she would look like Mye or some sort of monster, so I was surprised to see a woman walking to the door. Her eyes were the same size as ours. They were also brown, not purple like Mye's.

"Hi, I'm sorry about this," Mye's mom said.

"Don't be," my mom said.

Mye's mom invited us inside. She talked to Neal's dad and my mom while we played with Mye. He showed us toys that his species invented that were really cool. His computer also did neat things like floating in the air, and it would come to him when he called it. Of course it was much faster than our computers too.

As we played with Mye I thought about how glad I was to have him as a new friend. Less than an hour before, my friends and I didn't know much about Mye and unfairly judged him and his family. We let everything we knew about aliens get in the way. If we kept our beliefs, we would have never gotten to know him a little bit more. I was happy we didn't do that.

Max was sad to give us our homework back that day, but he did. I was shocked to see mine. I thought it was torn up. Mye explained that he made copies and ripped the homework to get our attention. I blushed when Mye said he liked my story.

Later on, our parents also called Mrs. King and talked to her and the principals at our school. In the end, the second homework assignment was cancelled and the aliens were allowed to come to school. At first only a few came. When they heard people were excited to have them there, and the alien kids were happier, a lot of aliens came out of hiding.

Max ended up being grounded for taking our papers. He had to also tell all of the kids that he was sorry and explained that he loved reading homework. After his punishment was over, the school gave Max a job as the teacher's helper. He was so excited that he got to help the teachers grade everyone's homework.

10.

A few months later Mye, Catalina, Tyrone, Neal, and I were walking to find our parents' cars after we got out of school.

"So, are you happy that you have to go to school now?" I asked.

"Is it all that you dreamed?" Catalina said.

"Well, maybe I should have said I just want to be able to come to recess," Mye said.

We laughed.

"That would have been best," Neal said.

"And lunch," Mye said.

"Only on Fridays, pizza day," Catalina said.

"Yep," I said.

"And game day," Neal said.

"Another one," Mye said.

"But then," Tyrone said, turning around to face us as he walked.

"Then what?" Catalina asked.

"Then everyone would be suspicious of him," Tyrone said. "He would be like Ollan on *Strange Things*—"

"Tyrone!" we said.

Thanks for reading!
Thanks to Faith Van Horne
for editing! Thanks to my
beta readers!

Join M. Mitnsi's mailing list
for updates on new releases:

http://eepurl.com/bwlw-P

AND

Check out the website:

http://mmitns.wix.com/mitnsi

About the Author

M. Mitnsi loved to write stories and poems at a younger age. After going to a lot of school, Mitnsi returned to writing. In off time, Mitinsi likes to explore science fiction, paranormal, and fantasy stories. This is Mitnsi's first children's book.

CPSIA information can be obtained at www.ICGtesting.com
Printed in the USA
LVOW11s0813160116

470900LV00001B/5/P